ELVIS
Man & Myth

ELVIS
Man & Myth

Sarah Parker Danielson

Designed by Tom Debolski

Edited and captioned by Marie Cahill

Page 1: **The King. Throughout his life he changed the world, and even now continues to do so.**
Previous page: **Quintessential Elvis—sexy, dynamic, charming.**
These pages, from left to right: **Elvis through the years—as a hot recording star for RCA; with Mary Ann Mobley in *Harum Scarum*; as Mike Edwards in *It Happened at the World's Fair*; as Jess Wade in *Charro!*, one of his last films.**

Contents

MIKE EDWARDS

Prologue

He was a country boy, born in East Tupelo, Mississippi, yet he would become not only the King of Rock and Roll, but *also* the King of the Hollywood romantic comedy. By 1956 Elvis Presley had left his indelible mark on the world of music. While continuing to please his rock and roll fans, he found a new avenue for his energy and naturally turned to Hollywood, the land where dreams and myths are made—and broken.

Producer Hal Wallis, the man behind such Hollywood classics as *Casablanca* and *The Maltese Falcon*, recognized the raw talent of a Marlon Brando (or perhaps a Richard Burbage—the premiere actor of Shakespeare's day) in Elvis and signed him to a seven-year contract.

Elvis would play a range of roles, but is best remembered for his early movies, in which he often played the part of the young rebel. For instance, in *King Creole*—under the guidance of Michael Curtiz, the Academy Award winning director of *Casablanca*—Elvis gave a memorable performance as Danny Fisher, a young drop-out who rose above the temptations of a life of crime.

The majority of Elvis' movies, however, found him cast as a variation on a character not unlike that of the great Valentino, a gregarious and self-assured man, constantly surrounded by a bevy of beautiful girls. As to be expected from a star who has influenced popular music as he had, most of the movies were musicals. Given their diverse settings, it is not surprising to find Elvis singing in a wide spectrum of places and situations. For example, in just one film—*GI Blues*—Elvis sang in beer gardens, on cable cars and trains. He sang to the Army, to children, even to a puppet. While certain critics maligned the songs, seeing little purpose or value in them compared to his early rock classics from 1954 to 1956, *every* Elvis soundtrack album was a bestseller.

Facing page: **Elvis, the King of Rock and Roll, parades across the grounds of Graceland—his Camelot. He would soon become the King of the Hollywood romantic comedy.**

To give perspective, almost all of Shakespeare's plays have music, and it always creates a mood. Beyond that, music is absolutely central to opera, musical revues, the Broadway musical and the Hollywood musical comedy. The music in Elvis Presley's films always had a carefully crafted *raison 'd'être*, with honorable antecedents going back to the choruses of the classic Greek drama. In fact, the movies of Elvis Presley are closely related to the operatic form. On the surface, the songs seem to be merely a convenient way to showcase the talent of the King of Rock and Roll. Yet on a deeper level, the songs are an integral part of each movie in that they advance the plot just as the score of a great opera expresses the story. Furthermore, on a purely emotional level, song—whether in a movie or an opera—adds to the richness of a dramatic tale.

The movies of Elvis Presley provide a key to the man himself—they are the canvas on which the myth of Elvis is painted. By studying the brushstrokes, we enlarge our understanding of the man, for the movies follow the progression of Elvis' own life. In his early movies he plays a young rebel, uncertain of who he is and where he is going. The movies of the middle years depict a man who is self-assured—until the proverbial midlife crisis hits. The man of the documentaries, the mature man who emerges from the crisis of fading youth has his confidence restored. He has taken what is best from his past and made it even better.

These pages: **With a string of successful musical comedies behind him, Elvis returned triumphantly to live performances with his** *NBC TV Special.* **He emerged stronger—even better—than before.**

Man & Myth

lvis' first film was *Love Me Tender* (1956), a Twentieth Century-Fox release of November 1956. A period piece, it has its setting in the Civil War era. Elvis received third billing, but ironically it was Elvis who was the main attraction. Panned by the critics, *Love Me Tender* was a smash at the box office. The critics could see only a rock star masquerading as an actor. What they failed to see was a young untried actor giving a better than credible performance. By quickly dismissing the movie as a B grade melodrama, the critics missed seeing a timeless and tragic love story. The fact that *Love Me Tender* is a period piece only serves to reinforce the timelessness of its theme.

Love Me Tender features Elvis as Clint Reno, the youngest of the four Reno brothers. Clint stays home to tend to the family farm in Texas during the Civil War, while his brothers join the Confederate Army. Clint's oldest brother, Vance (Richard Egan), is allegedly killed. Vance's presumed death paves the way for Clint to romance and marry Vance's sweetheart, Cathy (Debra Paget), whom Clint has always secretly loved. In the tradition of classical tragedy, this story of starcrossed love is bound to end in death.

The canon of world literature is filled with love stories of this sort, from Lancelot and Guinevere of Arthurian legend to Tristan and Isolde. Tristan and Isolde are especially pertinent. Their story began as a legend, and has been told in a variety of forms by a number of poets since medieval times, achieving its highest form in the opera, *Tristan und Isolde* by Richard Wagner.

Wagner tells the story of the knight Tristan, who is conducting the Princess Isolde to Cornwall to marry his uncle, King Mark. During the voyage the two fall in love. Both *Love Me Tender* and *Tristan und Isolde* revolve around the inevi-

Facing page: Elvis launched his film career with *Love Me Tender*, a classic love story set during the Civil War. He played Clint Reno, a character molded in the tradition of such tragic figures as Shakespeare's Romeo and Tristan from Arthurian legend.

Above: Like the heroes of so many classic love stories, young Clint's love leads to his death. *Right:* The star-crossed lovers— Clint and Cathy (Debra Paget). *Facing page:* Clint and Cathy share a poignant moment. Tragically, their happiness was short-lived, but their story would live on in the canon of great tragedies.

13

Above: Elvis as Deke Rivers in *Loving You*, a film that explores a young man's coming of age. As the film opens, Elvis plays a loner who delivers beer for a living. He joins a band, assuming only a minor role, but soon becomes a full-fledged member of the band and finally the main attraction. Along the way he must deal with a crisis of self.

table and often tragic complications of a love triangle. In *Love Me Tender*, Vance was not killed in the war as everyone believes, and his return sparks a feud between the brothers, ending in Clint's death. Similarly, in *Tristan und Isolde* the conflict between King Mark and Tristan leads to Tristan's death.

While *Love Me Tender* was a romantic period piece, Elvis' second film would look at life in a contemporary setting. *Loving You* (Paramount, July 1957) was the first of Elvis' movies that dealt with the theme of troubled youth. In *Loving You*, Elvis plays Deke Rivers, a young man who one day is delivering beer and the next is on the road with a country western band. Deke is soon catapulted to fame in much the same way that Elvis himself was.

The movie chronicles how Deke's rise to fame affects his personal development—and how, like the mythological figure Icarus, he is in danger of flying too high, too fast and too close to the sun. On one hand, *Loving You* is a contemporary story, offering a semi-realistic (Deke is perhaps too nice, too refined; even when he fights it is the other guy's fault and he is therefore exonerated) look at that modern day phenomenon—the rock star, and thus it is about Elvis himself and is an attempt to explain the myth behind the man.

But there is also a timelessness about this film in much the same sense that there is about *Love Me Tender*. There is

a difference, however. *Loving You* explores the eternal theme of a youth's coming of age and his struggles with himself. In essence, the movie is a *Bildungsroman* and as such tells the story of a sensitive young man trying to understand himself. The archetypal *Bildungsroman* is Goethe's *Wilhelm Meister*, although a more contemporary example is James Joyce's *A Portrait of the Artist as a Young Man*. The latter provides a particularly apt comparison to *Loving You* because Deke, like *Portrait's* Stephen Dedalus, the protagonist of Joyce's novel, must come to an understanding of his destiny as an artist.

Having taken his name—and in many ways, his identity—from a name carved on a gravestone, Deke is truly unsure of who he is—'I don't know anything more about him than I do me.' In his quest for understanding, he must also learn the ways of the world. Deke is initially unaware that his press agent—'Miss Glenda' as he respectfully calls her—is really a barracuda who has manipulated Deke in order to cash in on his rise to the top. At one point, when Deke begins to see the deception, and glimpses where life is taking him, he declares, 'I'm not so sure I like where I'm going.' By the film's conclusion, Deke has discovered who he is and what he wants out of life. In short, Deke has experienced an epiphany, a moment of insight in which reality is intuitively grasped. In contrast to the cynicism of Joyce's Stephen Dedalus—who has concluded that he must withdraw from family, friends and country—Deke realizes that he must stop running and embrace those around him.

Above: As *Loving You* draws to a conclusion, Deke has come to terms with what he wants out of life. His conflicts—both internal and external—are resolved. He has at last realized that he can stop running.

Of all of Elvis' films *Loving You* is the most autobiographical. Both Elvis and Deke were loners when they started out; Elvis, like Deke, was a truck driver before he found success as a singer, and success for both of them was met with both intense fan approval and stinging cultural criticism. In both cases, parents as well as civic and church leaders, cried that the young singing sensation was corrupting the morals of the other youth and must be stopped. Elvis' raw, sexual energy is symbolized by the guitar strings Deke breaks in the heat of performance. The audience reaction to Deke mirrors the crowd's response to Elvis on stage. Everyone is in a frenzy.

The autobiographical elements alone were enough to draw people to see *Loving You*. Because it starred Elvis, who by this time was a legend in his own time, *Loving You* did not have to be good to make money. Even so, *Loving You* can stand on its own merits. The movie's excitement lies not only in the myth of the man himself, but also in the universal tale of a youth's coming of age.

Made at the height of Elvis' recording career, *Jailhouse Rock* (MGM, October 1957) continues in the same vein as *Loving You*. Both are tales of a rebellious youth who rises above his ignoble past. *Jailhouse Rock* can be appreciated on a number of different levels. At its most basic level, the film provides a showcase for a great performer. The *Jailhouse Rock* song and dance sequence is a

Opposite page: In 1957, Elvis starred in *Jailhouse Rock*, a film that can be appreciated on a number of levels, offering exciting song and dance numbers and a thrilling plot. Beyond the action, however, lies a deeper meaning, for it is a classic story of the destructive forces of greed. *Below:* A barroom brawl has unforeseen implications (see the next page) for Vince Everett (Elvis), the protagonist of *Jailhouse Rock*.

Above: Vince is sent to prison for manslaughter for his part in the fight. While in jail, he shares a cell with Hunk Houghton (Mickey Shaugnessy), a former country-western singer who teaches Vince how to sing. Vince ultimately finds fame and fortune as a singer, but glory has a price, and he risks losing all that really matters.

slick production number choreographed by Elvis himself. The fast-paced plot belongs to that genre of entertaining stories that never fail to delight moviegoers with a happy ending—for at the film's conclusion the hero has resolved his personal problems and love shines on him and his beloved. Whereas Deke Rivers of *Loving You* is sweet and vulnerable, the protagonist of *Jailhouse Rock* is mean and egotistical. Elvis Presley gives a gripping performance as Vince Everett, a young punk who, while defending a woman, kills a man in a barroom brawl. Vince is jailed for manslaughter, and while in prison, he not only learns some of life's harder lessons, as in a flogging scene that reflects the corporal punishments visited on sailors in Richard Henry Dana's *Two Years Before the Mast*, but he also discovers he can sing.

Although the critics dismissed the film as the simple story of a country boy who makes good, such an analysis ignores the film's deeper meanings, for it is a classic story of the destructive forces of greed and ambition. It is the resolution of Vince's internal conflicts, however, that gives *Jailhouse Rock* its most complex dimension. Like the protagonist in any great literary work, the character of Vince has a tragic flaw. So caught up is he in making money that he is ready to forsake everything else. When love interest Peggy (Judy Tyler) asks Vince if money is all that matters, Vince—foolishly—tells her yes. Because of his greed, Vince risks losing all that is important to him—his friendship with former cellmate Hunk Houghton (Mickey Shaughnessy) and his

Above: **After his release from prison, Vince meets Peggy Van Alden (Judy Tyler). She never stops believing in him, but Vince becomes frustrated when fame is not immediate. Like many tragic characters—from King Midas to Macbeth—he demands too much.**

relationship with Peggy. Therein lies one of the strengths of Presley's films. The characters he portrays are people that his audience can immediately relate to—they have the human foibles that haunt so many of us. Vince is arrogant, mean, selfish and, above all, greedy.

Greed is one of the great tragic flaws, and has haunted the protagonists of many works of great literature. From the universally-known tale of King Midas to the works of that great tragic dramatist William Shakespeare, and from the great Wagnerian operas to such twentieth-century cinematic masterpieces as *Giant* and *Citizen Kane*, greed is the motivator for a wide variety of tragic actions. For instance, in the Wagnerian opera, *Das Rheingold*, Alberich renounces love forever so that he can become lord of all the world. Like Alberich, Vince renounces love in his quest for success. Only when Vince admits that he can feel love does he rescue himself from the snares of his greed, but that admittance does not come easily. This realization literally must be beaten into him. Alarmed by the manner in which Vince so carelessly tramples on Peggy's feelings, Hunk starts a fight. But Vince refuses to return the blows because he cannot bring himself to hit his old friend. Egotistical up to this point, Vince has finally come to an understanding of his inner self. With Vince's internal conflicts resolved, *Jailhouse Rock* avoids the tragic conclusion so often wrought by the excesses of greed.

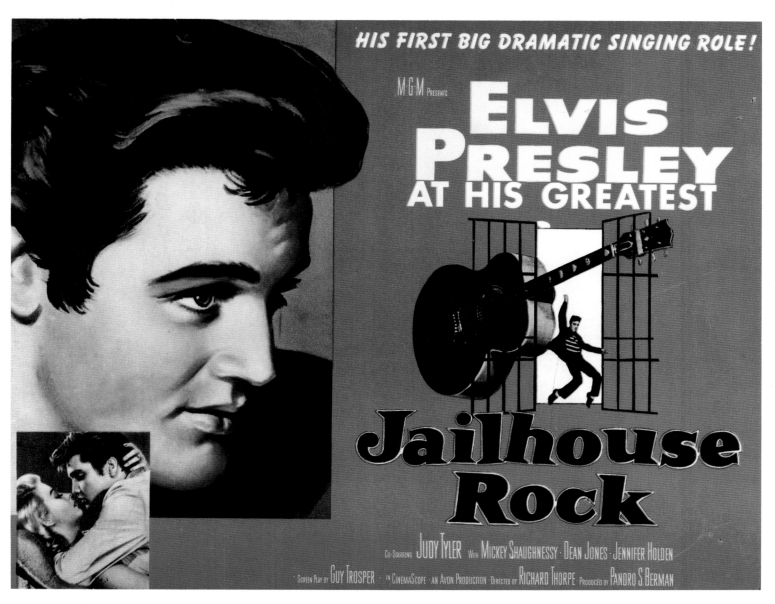

HIS FIRST BIG DRAMATIC SINGING ROLE!

M·G·M Presents

ELVIS PRESLEY AT HIS GREATEST

Jailhouse Rock

Co-Starring JUDY TYLER With MICKEY SHAUGHNESSY · DEAN JONES · JENNIFER HOLDEN

Screen Play by GUY TROSPER · in CinemaScope · An Avon Production · Directed by RICHARD THORPE · Produced by PANDRO S. BERMAN

Above: A poster advertising *Jailhouse Rock.* Although he had received only third billing for his first film, *Love Me Tender,* it did not take Hollywood long to realize Elvis' drawing power. *Left:* Elvis and Judy Tyler in a still from *Jailhouse Rock.*

Jailhouse Rock was heralded as Elvis' first dramatic singing role, but it is also noteworthy for Elvis' choreography of the *Jailhouse Rock* dance routine—a flamboyant, elaborately staged number *(these pages)*. The song is one of Elvis' all-time greatest hits, and remains a rock-and-roll classic to this day.

The movie is thus a tragi-comedy, in the style of Shakespeare's *Cymbeline* and *The Winter's Tale*. As is characteristic of this genre, the plot, theme and tone have the markings of a tragedy, and the action seems to be leading to a tragic conclusion—Vince could lose Peggy—but the turn of events leads to a happy outcome. Far more than the tale of an ex-con who strikes it rich, *Jailhouse Rock* explores the complexities of human nature in the best tradition of the greatest writers and philosophers.

K*ing Creole* (Paramount, May 1958) provides an even more compelling study of human nature. It is remembered as one of Elvis Presley's best movies, and in fact is probably the only one that was ever taken seriously by the critics. Like *Loving You*, it is a story in the *Bildungsroman* 'coming of age' tradition, but instead of the technicolor optimism that permeates *Loving You, King Creole* has the gritty realism of *film noir*. In *King Creole*, Elvis plays a rebellious young man tottering on the brink between good and evil. As he sings early in the movie, 'I never looked for trouble, but I never ran.' Set in New Orleans, the mood of the film effectively captures the seedy, sleazy yet somehow captivating essence of the Crescent City.

As is the case with *Loving You*, this film also parallels the personal life of Elvis. Elvis really *was* a disaffected southern youth who made it good. Just so is Danny Fisher, the protagonist of the film. Like Elvis, Danny has to work to help

Opposite page: Elvis as Danny Fisher with co-star Carolyn Jones in a publicity still for *King Creole*, regarded by many as Elvis' best film. In the scene *below*, Danny, a bus boy, meets Maxie Fields (Walter Matthau), a mobster who tries to humiliate Danny by demanding that he sing for the night club.

Above: In this still from *King Creole*, Elvis as Danny is flanked by the two women in his life—Dolores Hart on the left and Carolyn Jones on the right, representing, respectively, good and evil. Ronnie, the character played by Miss Jones, is a victim of circumstance. When she meets Danny, she tries to overcome her sordid past, but tragically she cannot escape. She is killed by Maxie.

support the family. In spite of his devotion to his family, Danny has lost his respect for his father (Dean Jagger): never will he let people walk over him as he believes they do his father.

These circumstances open up the encyclopedia of human emotions: loyalty, greed, love, hate. Above all, *King Creole* focuses on the age-old theme of good versus evil. Throughout the movie, these are almost continually juxtaposed. Charlie, the good but poor owner of the King Creole night club, provides a contrast to the evil but wealthy Maxie Fields (Walter Matthau), who runs just about everything else on Bourbon Street. Maxie is evil incarnate, a modern day Iago, who willingly destroys anyone who interferes with him. Charlie, on the other hand, wants what is best for Danny. Nellie (Dolores Hart), Danny's sweet girlfriend, plays the foil to Ronnie (Carolyn Jones), the not-so-sweet mistress of Maxie Fields. The characters avoid becoming mere caricatures of good and evil because Ronnie is not completely bad, nor is Nellie completely good. To complicate matters even further, Danny is drawn to both women, but cannot yet love either one until he figures out who he is.

The conflict between good and evil crystallizes most clearly within Danny himself. Like Don Quixote in Cer-

Above: **The glimmer of a switch blade against the backdrop of a dark shadow symbolizes the struggle that emerges between good and evil in *King Creole*, especially in the character of Danny.**

vantes' sixteenth century masterpiece, he is a bit confused, and finds himself challenging illusory ogres while the very real ones that are all around him nearly eat him up. Danny wants to please his father but refuses to go back to school, relenting only when his father finds a job. He wants to follow his father's wishes and stay in school, but Charlie's offer of $85 a week is too tempting to refuse. Though his intentions are good, his actions are criminal. Because he is upset by the way in which his father's boss browbeats his father, Danny agrees to join Maxie's thugs and beat up the owner. He then changes his mind, but it is too late to avert trouble. The wrong man is mugged and his father winds up on the operating table. For the moment, evil has triumphed.

As the film progresses, it meanders into the realm of the sentimental and the melodramatic. Overall, however, *King Creole* works. The mixture of ethos and pathos has garnered the audience's sympathy. Elvis was reportedly more pleased with the positive reviews he received for *King Creole* than he was with anything else in his career. If Elvis wanted to be remembered as an actor, this was certainly a step in the right direction, but life often moves in unexpected directions. After *King Creole*, Elvis Presley's film career came to a temporary halt with his induction in to the Army. The films that followed his military service would have a decidedly different texture than King Creole and the others that came before.

GI Blues (Paramount, October 1960), Elvis' first film after his stint in the Army, is a marked departure from his earlier films. It is the beginning of Elvis' transition from the bad boy rock and roller of the late 1950s to the well-groomed balladeer that he would come to be in the 1960s. Fearful that his fans had forgotten him, Elvis set out to capture a broader audience.

Critics decried GI Blues, claiming that Elvis had sold out, that he had embraced the middle-of-the-road audience, and in doing so had cheapened himself. What is often forgotten is the lesson that dramatists and audiences throughout the ages have always known: a work of art for a popular audience has to have a greater sense of immediacy. It must have a universality to it that makes it accessible to all. Though the settings evoke a particular time, the theme must transcend time. People today not only sympathize with Moliere's character, the Hypochondriac, in the sharp satire of the same name, but the Hypochondriac now lives next door. Five hundred years from now, the same may well be said of Elvis' movies.

GI Blues, like many of Elvis' later films, bears a striking similarity to the comedies of William Shakespeare, particularly Much Ado About Nothing and The Comedy of Errors. Like these plays, the plot is advanced through a series of

Elvis Presley as a real-life soldier (below) and in GI Blues (facing page), his first film after two years in the army. Something had changed: GI Blues was unlike any other film Elvis had made. In retrospect, it clearly signalled the beginning of a new period of film-making, one that was characterized by a suave, self-assured leading man who had left behind youth's turmoils.

complicated twists and misunderstandings. The plot of *GI Blues* revolves around a bet that Tulsa (Elvis), a young soldier stationed in Germany, has with his Army buddies. The bet calls for him to persuade Lili (Juliet Prowse), a beautiful cabaret singer, to spend the night with him. Tulsa of course falls in love with her and she with him, but Lili puts a stop to the blossoming romance when she learns of the bet, believing that Tulsa has deceived her. As with most Shakespearean comedies, *GI Blues* is the story of love almost gone awry. At the basis of this tangled love affair is one of Shakespeare's most pervasive themes—appearance versus reality. As is illustrated again and again in Shakespeare, reality is not always what it seems. Tulsa appears to have deceived Lili. In reality, he really does love her. The conflict cannot be resolved until Lili is able to distinguish appearance from reality. *GI Blues* can thus be interpreted as a modern rendering of Shakespeare's *Much Ado About Nothing*, with a role reversal casting Elvis in the part of Hero, the falsely accused maiden. At the conclusion of *Much Ado*, the principal characters have learned the difference between what is and what merely appears to be, and love one another with a love based on reality rather than on mere appearance and outward form. This conclusion is clearly the forerunner to that of *GI Blues*.

Opposite page: In *GI Blues*, Elvis played Tulsa MacLean, a soldier stationed in Germany. *Above left:* In a manner reminiscent of Shakespeare's comedies, the plot involves a number of complicated twists and romantic entanglements. *Above:* Juliet Prowse plays Lili, Elvis' romantic interest. Despite the problems encountered along the way, by the film's conclusion, the two characters have learned the difference between what *is* and what merely *appears to be*, and thus can acknowledge their love for each other.

In *Flaming Star*, Elvis played Pacer Burton, a character modeled on the heroes of the Old West. Like those men, Pacer struggles to restore order to a chaotic world. *Above:* Elvis and two of his co-stars from the film, Steve Forrest and Barbara Eden.

The theme of appearance versus reality recurs in many of Elvis' later films, and it is a theme which wove its way through his own life as well: his fans demanded that Elvis play a certain kind of role, one they equated with Elvis himself. The reality of the man, however, did not fit the image his fans had created for him. Box office receipts provide irrefutable evidence that people wanted to see Elvis as Tulsa rather than as Pacer Burton, the serious character he played in *Flaming Star* (Twentieth Century-Fox, December 1960), his next film. By this time Elvis was so firmly enmeshed in the myth surrounding him that his fans rebelled if he stepped out of the carefully crafted persona of the *GI Blues* mold.

In *Flaming Star* Elvis tried a different sort of film, this time a tragedy dealing with the futility and stupidity of war. Elvis is Pacer Burton, a man torn between two worlds—the Indian world of his mother, and the white world of his father. When war breaks out between the Indians and the whites, Pacer finds himself in the middle of the conflict, literally as well as emotionally. Like Shakespeare's Hamlet, Pacer is torn by familial loyalties. Pacer is a character not unlike Elvis himself—moody and hot-tempered but with an undeniable presence. Both men are outsiders. Pacer belongs to neither the white man's world nor the Indian's world; Elvis, in spite of all his adoring fans and friends, is a man alone.

War and prejudice will soon wipe out the happy mood portrayed *above*. Throughout the film, prejudice is interwoven with the theme of love. Barbara Eden, *left*, who plays Pacer's fiancee, is unwilling to accept Pacer's Indian relatives.

Flaming Star also has its roots in the stories of King Arthur, the legend of Robin Hood and (closer to home) the tales of the American West—all of which represent the monumental struggles of individuals to restore order in the face of chaos and anarchy. The Old West has been a major source of American romance since the nineteenth century. The plots typically follow a simple formula: The hero, with horse and gun, defends justice against a villain. *Flaming Star* takes this simple formula to new heights. Although it is easy distinguish between the good guys and the bad, the real villain is prejudice. Despite his valiant efforts, Pacer cannot overpower man's inhumanity to man. Prejudice runs too deep, and the film ends tragically. Like Billy Budd in Herman Melville's classic tale, Pacer Burton is an unusually pure, unsullied man—and this very purity is doomed for destruction by the evil forces of the world.

Flaming Star was followed by *Wild in the Country* (Twentieth Century-Fox, June 1961), another drama. Elvis as Glen Tyler is once again cast as an angry young man. As he was in his pre-Army films, he is rebellious—an outsider confused about what he wants out of life. The theme of the rogue, the man on the outside of society can be traced back to ancient Rome and Petronius' *Satyricon*. By the sixteenth century, such 'rogue' literature became a definite form, the picaresque novel. The central figure, or *picaro*, lives by his wits, getting into and out of

In ***Wild in the Country***, **Glen Tyler (Elvis) is involved with three women, each one representing one aspect of his personality. Tuesday Weld *(below)* as Noreen represents the rebellious side, whereas Hope Lange *(facing page)* as Glen's therapist Irene is symbolic of his struggle to understand himself. Millie Perkins (not shown) plays Betty Lee, who represents the past.**

Below: A soulful Elvis. Throughout his acting career, Elvis demonstrated that he could play a range of emotions. *Right:* The struggles burning within Glen Tyler are not evident in this quiet, family scene from *Wild in the Country*.

trouble. Glen Tyler is a twentieth-century *picaro*. Like Henry Fielding's unforgettable Tom Jones, Glen is often on the wrong side of the law. Finally, Glen comes to a turning point in his life: He can go to prison, or with the help of a therapist, he can sort out who he is and what he wants out of life.

Made at a transitional point in his career, *Wild in the Country* mirrors the confusion that Elvis felt about the direction his career should take. From a strictly financial point of view, the lightweight musical comedies, such as *GI Blues,* were the most rewarding. *Blue Hawaii* and *Viva Las Vegas,* both of which followed *Wild in the Country,* were his two biggest money makers. However, to be continually cast as the smiling, guitar-strumming charmer would mean that the critics could never take him seriously as an actor. His movies never earned him an Oscar nomination, but if success can be measured by the reaction of the general public, Elvis' movies were a tremendous success. A major criticism of Elvis' movies is that, generally, they evidence very little originality of thought. The same can be said of much of the world's great literature. The ancient Greeks dealt with love, greed, pride—the full catalogue of human emotions. Shakespeare is among the best known writers who 'borrowed' his ideas from previous writings. These so-called borrowings certainly do not make Shakespeare any less of a playwright and poet. The issues Shakespeare probed in his writings were as meaningful in his day as they were in the time of the ancient Greeks and Romans—and their importance is no less diminished today. Man is still trying to understand the

Elvis' fans wanted him to—and in a sense, insisted that he—play the charming, self-confident man *(opposite page)*, rather than the struggling, uncertain Glen in *Wild in the Country*. *Above:* Elvis rehearses off-stage with Tuesday Weld.

subtleties of the human psyche, and Elvis' movies are yet another in a long and honorable line of vehicles for that exploration.

Wild in the Country is a prime example of how an individual is often forced to explore his (or her) own psyche. Glen (Elvis) is torn between the women in his life, and he also faces a struggle between his own wild, rebellious nature and his desire to better himself. This story of one individual is hauntingly familiar precisely because it partakes of the universal experience of mankind. That is why *Wild in the Country* or any of Elvis' movies work—they tap into our collective unconscious.

With *Blue Hawaii* (Paramount, November 1961), the trend that had begun with *GI Blues* was now firmly set. The mood of *Blue Hawaii*, and of the movies that were to follow was fun in the sun—featuring a nice, fun-loving guy surrounded by pretty girls and pretty scenery and singing lots of songs. That *Blue Hawaii* is what is often termed 'a comedy' only adds to its classic overtones—for the very root of the word comedy comes from the Greek for 'musical revel,' an apt description for this genre of Elvis' films.

In *Blue Hawaii* Elvis Presley becomes Chad Gates, the rebellious son of a pineapple tycoon. Chad's rebelliousness has its roots in his need to make his own way in the world.

Blue Hawaii **was one of Elvis' biggest money makers. Although it is a musical comedy, the film has serious underpinnings, as seen in this still of a reflective Elvis** *(opposite page)*. **Of course,** *Blue Hawaii* **is not without its lighter moments** *(below)*.

Much like Elvis himself, Chad is expected to be and act a certain way. Beneath the pineapple fluff, *Blue Hawaii* has the flavor of the pre-*GI Blues* movies. In spite of its light-hearted trappings, *Blue Hawaii*, though very different in tone from *King Creole* or *Wild in the Country* (which used a grim and somber tone to convey the thematic seriousness), explores a similar theme—a disaffected youth in search of himself. *Blue Hawaii* could never be called somber, yet this romantic comedy nonetheless explores the serious.

Humor has always been an effective means for conveying a serious theme: writers, from the dramatists of ancient Greece to the postmodernists of today use humor, even parody, to avoid sentimentality, and thereby prevent an overly emotional reaction from becoming a substitute for an intellectual response. For example, in John Barth's *Chimera*, Bellerophon is a parody of the mythic hero Perseus. At one point, he finds himself in the unhappy (but humorous to the reader) situation of owning a Pegasus who cannot fly. Underneath the humor, Barth is addressing the serious theme of an individual's ability to adapt and therefore survive. In a similar manner, *Blue Hawaii* brilliantly avoids the sentimental by using romantic entanglements and other humorous misunderstandings.

Though scorned by the critics, Elvis' musical comedies were tremendously popular with his fans. The enormous success of these films was due in part to the public's percep-

Below: *Blue Hawaii* **is filled with a bevy of sun-bathing beauties—a characteristic that would persist throughout Elvis' later films.** *Facing page:* **Elvis as Chad Gates with one of his many romantic interests.**

tion of Elvis. His fans equated the roles he played with the man himself. It is true, however, that a number of parallels can be drawn between *Blue Hawaii* and Elvis' personal life. Certainly Elvis, like Chad Gates, had the air of rebellion about him, as was evidenced by the black clothes and side burns he sported in the 1950s—an era when nearly everyone else wore crewcuts.

Who was this man we called the King? Ensconced as he was behind the walls of Graceland—his Camelot—did we ever really understand him?

As King, was his duty first to us, his loyal subjects, or to himself?

Elvis was certainly compelled by his public to star in a certain kind of role. Ironically, as he made thrice annual journeys from Memphis to Hollywood, Elvis' life would become imitative of his movies. His Hollywood years were undeniably years of glamour, of beautiful women and fast cars, but it was glamour without substance. His life had become a parody of his movie roles. Beyond Hollywood, Elvis had no life—he had stopped touring and his recordings were almost exclusively tied to his films. His life was less real than his films. The easy-going, self-assured minstrel of the movies was, in reality, shy and aloof. Elvis was a desperate recluse sheltered from the world by Graceland, a parody in itself, with only Priscilla and his father to coax him into the sunlight.

As Elvis' Hollywood career boomed, he became more and more wary of the public, taking refuge at Graceland *(below)* between films. Eventually, Pygmalion would take a bride *(facing page)*— Priscilla Beaulieu, whom he had kept guarded behind the walls of Graceland for four years before their marriage.

fter *Blue Hawaii* came *Follow That Dream* (United Artists, March 1962), with Elvis again singing, romancing pretty girls and saving the day. As in *Blue Hawaii*, the emphasis is on comedy with serious underpinnings. The movie explores the age old issue of right versus might—a theme that has its roots in Arthurian legend. In the movie, City Hall represents might, while Elvis and his family represent right.

Elvis turned from the comedic to the overtly dramatic with *Kid Galahad* (United Artists, July 1962), a remake of the old Humphrey Bogart–Edward G Robinson film. It is a serious look at a young boxer's rise to fame, and it takes Elvis out of the mold in which the public has cast him. Trapped in his public persona he returns to the light-hearted musical with *Girls! Girls! Girls!* (Paramount, November 1962). This film explores the age-old theme of family loyalty. In *Girls! Girls! Girls!*, Ross Carpenter (Elvis) is motivated by the desire to reclaim his family's sailboat, which was lost when financial woes struck.

The Elvis of the romantic comedies was different from Elvis we had known before. His early films (*Loving You, Jailhouse Rock, King Creole, Wild in the Country*) dealt with rebellion and the struggle to discover oneself. They were about the search for identity. In contrast, the later films present a character who knows who he is. In fact, the later characters exude self-confidence rather than indecision. They are smooth-talking men, not boys plagued by life's turmoils: Hamlet has grown up.

Below: **Elvis behind the wheel of one of his treasured autos.** *Opposite page: Kid Galahad,* **a drama, was a departure from the type of films that Elvis' fans preferred to see him in, and as such did not do as well at the box office.**

As Elvis himself matured, so too did his characters. Iron-ically, the critics saw this shift as a regression. The confi-dence that replaced youthful indecision is falsely interpreted as shallowness. In reality, what was happening was a logical progression symbolic of the development of an individual, namely Elvis himself.

Now that the boy is a man, the films change direction and are aimed toward the family. Some will even include children as an inte-gral element of the plot. *It Happened at the World's Fair* (MGM, April 1963), for example, features Elvis as babysitter for the better part of the film. As protagonist Mike Edwards, Elvis Presley bears little resemblance to the rebellious young men of his early films. Far from rebellious, Mike is the epitome of respon-sibility, taking it upon himself to care for seven-year-old Sue-Lin (Vicky Tiu) whose uncle has disappeared, and at the same time keeps his eye on his gambling, good-hearted but misguided partner Danny (Gary Lockwood). Though he and Danny are down on their luck and risk losing their airplane, Mike will take no part in a plan to smuggle furs across the Canadian border.

The characters Elvis now plays have gained respectability. And so too has Elvis himself. The wild and sensuous hip swaying belongs to the past. The King of Rock and Roll now sings a duet with a child or croons a ballad, guitar gently

Opposite page: **In contrast to the rebellious youth he played in** ***King Creole*** **or** ***Wild in the Country*,** **Elvis as Mike Edwards in** ***It Happened at the World's Fair*** **is the epitome of responsibility. He has become the family man. Indeed, in** ***It Happened at the World's Fair*,** **he is the self-appointed guardian of seven-year-old Sue-Lin, played by Vicky Tiu** *(above)*.

Elvis in his rockin' pre-army days *(above)* provides quite a contrast to the serious, mature persona of his movies, such as Mike Edwards in *It Happened at the World's Fair (facing page)*.

cradled in his arms. After his two years in the Army, he could never go home to rock and roll (or so it seemed). The metamorphosis was complete. Elvis, having left rock and roll behind him, became the family man, a younger version of the affable Fred MacMurray.

It Happened at the World's Fair is filled with symbolism befitting its optimistic tone. The setting is the 1962 Seattle World's Fair — what better icon for the promise of tomorrow. Finally recovered from World War II, the United States was caught up in the enthusiasm of its young and charismatic President Kennedy and his vision for a new frontier. With its theme — 'Man in the Space Age' — the Seattle World's Fair was part of that vision: John Glenn had just become the first American to orbit the earth, and the race to the moon was on.

The optimistic symbolism of the movie carries through to Mike's romantic interest: Diane (Joan O'Brien) is a nurse — a wholesome, nurturing occupation and one of the three acceptable careers for women in the early 1960s. She thus adhered to the prescriptions of society and would make a suitable wife for the King.

As a nurse, Diane, of course, wears white, the color of virgins. White is the color for brides and thus the optimistic symbolism is further reinforced. All of Elvis' leading ladies have been 'good girls,' but Nurse Diane is the epitome of goodness. (The one exception to the good girl rule is Ronnie in *King Creole*, but she dies, thus clearing the way for good girlfriend Nellie.)

Although at the beginning of the movie Elvis is a good-hearted playboy, we see what the right woman can do. In an early scene, a shotgun-toting father chases Elvis away from his daughter, whose name Elvis keeps forgetting. As the movie progresses, his attitude toward women changes. Under the influence of true love he becomes caring and sensitive, a precursor of the 'Eighties Man.' When he is not romancing Diane (and sometimes while he is), the thoughtful and responsible Mike/Elvis shares the screen with Sue-Lin, the little girl who depends on him to take care of her. In a conclusion drenched in All-American symbolism, Mike, with Diane on his arm, submits his application to NASA against the backdrop of a big parade. This happy ending closes with a song called—what else—'Happy Ending.'

For his next film, Elvis leaves Seattle behind for the sands of Acapulco. *Fun in Acapulco* (Paramount, November 1963) can be characterized as another fun-in-the-sun movie featuring plenty of bikini-clad girls. The tone and plot are typical of Elvis' other movies from this era. In the tradition of *Blue Hawaii*, there is an underlying seriousness to the film because it deals with how one must confront one's fears. Elvis plays Mike Wingren, a trapeze artist who, following a brush with death, is afraid of heights. Again, we see Elvis playing a character who must resolve his internal conflicts.

Below: Away from the public eye, Elvis could relax. Much of the time, however, he was trapped in his own myth—a figure larger than life. *Facing page:* The critics dismissed his movies as lightweight fluff, never recognizing the depth he brought to each role, which we can clearly see in this still from *Fun in Acapulco*.

issin' Cousins (MGM, March 1964), in which Elvis plays a dual role, is a film ripe with symbolism. The two Elvises represent the dichotomy that Elvis must have felt in his personal life. He was, after all, the man who had to live up to the myth of the one and only King of Rock and Roll—and yet his fans demanded that he star in movies that were as far removed as possible from that myth. In *Kissin' Cousins*, the two characters (Josh Morgan and Jodie Tatum) played by Elvis are pitted against each other, reinforcing the symbolism of Elvis' own internal conflicts. Josh Morgan is the young Army officer whose task it is to remove the Tatum family from their mountain home so that the government can install a military base. The hillbilly life of the Tatums brings to mind the unspoiled paradise Herman Melville described in his treatises on nineteenth-century natural paradises, *Omoo* and *Typee*. The Tatums themselves can be likened to Jean-Jacques Rousseau's Noble Savages, living in a natural sort of civilization, and carrying on animated conversations as full of intricate regional mannerisms as Eudora Welty's brilliant short story 'Why I Live at the PO.'

Who was Elvis? Had he come to believe that he was the suave hero he played in his Hollywood movies? Conflicts on film are notoriously easier to resolve than those in real life and in the movie the cousins settle their differences amicably. For Elvis, a victim of the mythology that had become his life, things were not so easily solved. The end of his Army career was the beginning of his seclusion. Wary of crowds yet never wanting to be alone, he would rent movie theatres

Kissin' Cousins **provides a keen psychological insight into Elvis, the man. Torn by his need to live up to the myth, Elvis was a man at odds with himself. The internal conflicts he struggled with are symbolized by the dual role he played in** *Kissin' Cousins*. *Below:* **One half of the pair of Elvises.**

Left: As Jodie Tatum, Elvis fought to retain the rights to his family's idyllic home. *Below:* The Tatums in their naturalistic setting.

for the amusement of himself and his ever-present entourage.

It was also during this period that Elvis had Priscilla Beaulieu sequestered at Graceland, living with him in a technically platonic relationship until their marriage. Unable to make a commitment to her, he nonetheless played a dual role with her, demanding she always be at his beck and call.

By the time that Elvis made *Viva Las Vegas* (MGM, April 1964), the critics had long dismissed him as a B-movie actor, claiming that he was simply walking through a series of movies with interchangeable plots. While that may sound like a denunciation, the movies are simply following a traditional pattern.

Romances have adhered to a set of specific conventions since the unknown poet of *Sir Gawain and the Green Knight* caught the fancy of medieval England. As the idealized hero of Old English epics gave way to a more realistic if somewhat less admirable man, a new kind of hero emerged, one not too far removed from the characters played by Elvis. The hero fights, laughs, cries, plays games and above all falls in and out of love. He is someone the reader/audience can sympathize with. The stories in which he appears revolve around a number of miscellaneous adventures with a few fights added for excitement. The plots of these stories make liberal use of the improbable; the characters are stock and

Opposite page: The character of Lucky in *Viva Las Vegas* can trace his antecedents back to the days of Sir Lancelot. *Above:* In this scene from *Viva Las Vegas*, Lucky does his best to interfere with Count Mancini's (Cesare Danova) attempts to woo Rusty (Ann-Margret).

Since medieval times, romances have adhered to a specific set of conventions. The plot requires a great deal of action as well as liberal use of the improbable. *Viva Las Vegas* supplies both. In the scene *above*, Rusty coaxes Lucky into joining her dance class. The result is the high energy *C'mon Everybody* sequence.

could be switched from one story (or movie) to another without creating too much of a disturbance in the basic narrative. Gawain, like Lancelot, is the most courteous, most valiant knight. Likewise, in spite of differences in their personalities, Johnny Tyronne in *Harum Scarum*, Rusty Wells in *Girl Happy* and Ted Jackson in *Easy Come, Easy Go* share many of the same basic characteristics. All are likable young men with a knack for attracting women, usually more women than they can handle.

In *Viva Las Vegas*, a modern day romance, action and adventure abound. Elvis and co-star Ann-Margret dance, shoot skeet, ride motorbikes, take part in a make-believe Wild West shoot-out, fly in a helicopter and water ski. And that is just in one day! Although this chain of events is improbable, the audience experiences what Samuel Taylor Coleridge refers to as a 'willing suspension of disbelief' and is caught up in action. This high sense of adventure gives a genuine excitement to the film.

Elvis' own life had a similar reliance on action. The circular driveway of Graceland became a racetrack for hundreds of go-cart races, and the hills outside Hollywood roared with the motorcycles of Elvis and his entourage. The myth surrounding Elvis had pumped him up larger than life.

Underneath this action-packed adventure story lies more substance than one would think. Elvis is again playing the smooth-talking, self-confident man about town, a race car driver named Lucky. This time, however, there is a difference. Lucky's feelings for Rusty (Ann-Margret) compel him to examine his life's priorities. In a manner reminiscent of

This page: Viva Las Vegas is regarded as one of Elvis' better musicals. In this film we see a leading character more introspective than in some of the other musicals, a change that is motivated by the romance between Lucky (Elvis) and Rusty (Ann-Margret).

the early Presley films, Lucky must learn to know himself. He is forced to explore the meaning of love, and in doing so, discovers that he needs somebody. *Viva Las Vegas* concludes with the wedding of Lucky and Rusty. Elvis' characterization is more introspective than typically seen in his films from this period. Perhaps Elvis himself was experiencing the need for re-assessing *his* life's priorities. Although his offscreen romance with Ann-Margret undoubtedly added some sizzle to the film, it damaged his relationship with Priscilla, who was waiting patiently for his return to Graceland.

An example of a movie that is taken from an earlier work of art is *Roustabout* (Paramount, November 1964). The movie is a modern day rendition of Richard Wagner's opera, *Die Meistersinger von Nürnberg*. Both the movie and the opera tell the story of a young man—an unknown whose singing talents are recognized

Below: **The setting of Richard Wagner's opera, *Die Meistersinger von Nurnberg* is transferred to a modern day carnival in *Roustabout*. Elvis plays Charlie Rogers, an updated version of the opera's Walther von Stolzing.**

and encouraged. In *Roustabout*, Elvis plays Charlie Rogers, a carnival jack-of-all-trades. Maggie Morgan (Barbara Stanwyck), the owner of the carnival, is willing to give Elvis his big chance to sing under the big top, but he faces opposition for his unusual style. In Wagner's opera, the townspeople object to protagonist Walter's entering their all-important singing contest, which he eventually wins. Both characters face opposition because they are unconventional. By the end of each story, however, the two characters have earned the respect that is their due.

I n 1965, Elvis continued the cycle of romantic comedies with a trilogy that included *Girl Happy*, *Tickle Me* and *Harum Scarum*. As is characteristic of the genre, all feature a great deal of action seasoning a series of improbable plots. The plot of *Girl Happy* (MGM, January 1965) revolves around the relationship between Rusty Wells (Elvis) and Valerie (Shelley Fabares). Following

Below: **As to be expected from a singer who had influenced popular music as he had, most of Elvis' movies were musicals. The three movies he released in 1965—*Girl Happy*, *Tickle Me* and *Harum Scarum*—were no exception.**

a string of improbabilities—mass arrests, barroom brawls and poolside dances—the central characters discover their true feelings for each other. Like the comedies of Shakespeare and, more recently, Gilbert and Sullivan, *Girl Happy* explores the meaning of love between two people as the most basic of all relationships.

Elvis' next film, *Tickle Me* (Allied Artists, June 1965) notwithstanding its silly name, is imbued with ideas that have occupied mankind since the dawn of intelligent thought. With Elvis playing Lonnie Beale, a rodeo buckaroo, there is action aplenty—and with the legend of a lost gold mine as its central motif, the film is a retelling of the quest for the Golden Fleece.

*T*hen came the surrealistic fun of *Harum Scarum* (MGM, December 1965). The element that one need not look for in the action of *Harum Scarum* is logic. To do so would be alien to the spirit of the film, for improbabilities are an accepted convention of romantic comedies. When Viola in Shakespeare's *Twelfth Night* wears a disguise that is identical to the clothing worn by her shipwrecked brother, we do not wonder how this could have come about. Likewise, when Johnny Tyronne (Elvis Presley) is kidnapped by a band of assassins so that he can assassinate a king we do not question the logic of such an improbable event.

Facing page: In *Harum Scarum*, Elvis is Johnny Tyronne, a character who bears a remarkable similarity to Rudolph Valentino's Sheik. Elvis himself is much like Valentino—both men have incredible power over their fans. *Above:* In between movies, Elvis still found time to devote to his first love—music.

Though not without a touch of satire, *Harum Scarum* should be remembered for what it is—a romantic fantasy. The Middle Eastern setting, with characters dressed as Hollywood's version of sheiks and slave girls, evokes an otherworldliness that captures the heart and the imagination. Elvis as Johnny Tyronne portrays a modern day Rudolph Valentino. Johnny, like Valentino, is a movie star capable of bringing his female fans to the edge of hysteria.

Elvis was eager to play the part of Johnny Tyronne because he identified it with Valentino's role in *The Sheik*. He not only saw the movie as an opportunity to create an interesting character but was fascinated by the physical similarities between himself and Valentino. Even beyond the physical similarities, Elvis is remarkably like Valentino. Both men had an incredible power over their fans, a power that stemmed from their eroticism. Their presence, whether on stage or on screen, was enough to turn a quiet group into a screaming throng. Both men were larger than life, but both were trapped in an image. Valentino's wife Natasha Rambova controlled his career in much the same way that Colonel Parker controlled Elvis'. Valentino's sudden death at the age of 31 created mass hysteria among his female fans, and thousands of women lined the streets during his funeral,

Below: **The King of the Hollywood romantic comedy between takes at the MGM studio.** *Facing page:* **Mary Ann Mobley joins Elvis in the romantic fantasy, *Harum Scarum*.**

causing a near riot. When Elvis died, countless people descended on Graceland to mourn and to pay their last respects. The devotion of their fans continued years after their deaths. Valentino fan clubs were as active after he died as they were during the height of his career. Today, the fans of Elvis buy his albums, watch his movies and make the pilgrimage to Graceland. Numerous books have been written about Elvis, and magazines and tabloids still feature articles on him. The myths that were spun during their lives have endured.

As with *opera buffa*, *Harum Scarum* interweaves merriment and drama with music. A parade of characters that includes orphans, the King of Thieves and a dwarf provide the merriment—and, although a comedy, the plot involves such serious themes as political intrigue, with brother pitted against brother, kidnappings and (of course) love. As to be expected, the music is supplied by Elvis, and because the audience is caught up in the fantasy, he can burst into song at the most improbable moments. Elvis sings and dances with the two young orphans in his care. As we saw in *It Happened at the World's Fair*, Elvis has evolved into a respectable and responsible young man, the sort a nice girl could bring home to meet mom and dad.

Facing page: In *Harum Scarum*, Elvis possesses all the requisite qualities of a romantic hero. In addition to being handsome, he is daring and, above all, willing to risk himself to save someone else—an endeavor at which he always succeeds. *Below:* Elvis' talent was so great that he transcended mere popularity and became a mythological figure.

ohnny (Elvis Presley) of *Frankie and Johnny* (United Artists, July 1966) has a few traits of which mom and dad would not approve: he is a gambler. Inspired by the old blues song, the movie revolves around the ancient themes of love and jealousy. 'Frankie and Johnny were lovers/Oh lordy how they could love/They swore to be true to each other/True as the stars above/He was her man/But he was doing her wrong.' In the movie Johnny believes his bad luck at cards will change if he is involved with a redhead. Frankie (Donna Douglas) is overcome with jealousy when she learns that Johnny, as the song says, 'was loving up Nellie Bly.' Jealousy frequently leads to tragic conclusions, as is in Ken Kesey's twentieth-century epic novel, *Sometimes a Great Notion*. In *Frankie and Johnny*, however, love is the dominant theme and the characters successfully overcome the same passion that is sweeping Hank and Leland Stamper to their destruction at the end of the Kesey novel.

Below: **In** *Frankie and Johnny*, **Elvis plays Johnny, a riverboat gambler, seen here at the roulette table, with Nellie Bly (Nancy Kovack) and Cully (Harry Morgan). Like** *Jailhouse Rock, Frankie and Johnny* **explores the consequences of greed.** *Facing page*: **Elvis will be forever immortalized by his recordings and in his films.**

With *Paradise Hawaiian Style* (Paramount, June 1966), Elvis Presley returned to the Hawaiian Islands—the Elysium of the twentieth century. Hawaii's archetypal sun-drenched beaches represent the ideal world—one of golden sand and beautiful people. It is as eerily idyllic as Alfred Tennyson's land of *The Lotos-Eaters*. In the tradition of the dream world, it is a magic land of escape, but instead of torpid castaways lounging out their days in an eternal narcotic haze, handsome surfers and bathing beauties frolic in the sands of an eternal summer. Like the sailors lured to Tennyson's pleasure-beclouded shore, these fun-loving young lovers have little to do but engage in fanciful intrigues and talk of love. Indeed, as Tennyson said, it is a land 'in which it seemed always afternoon.' There is an element of unreality to it all, but that is an accepted convention of the form. Likewise, the 'shepherds' of the English Renaissance pastoral plays spoke in courtly language and appeared in clothing better suited to drawing rooms than to rocky hills and swampy meadows. *Paradise Hawaiian Style* features such unrealistic elements as the preternaturally clean, well-groomed and handsome appear-

Below: **The pastoral plays of the English Renaissance were the forerunners to the idyllic world depicted in *Paradise Hawaiian Style*. Both portray magic lands of escape.**

ance of all characters in the film, and the inexplicable 'big production number,' complete with scores of native singers. Yet, to the audience, it does not seem unrealistic at all.

High adventure is the hallmark of Elvis' next two films: *Spinout* (MGM, December 1966) and *Easy Come, Easy Go* (Paramount, June 1967). Both are typical of Elvis' movies in particular, and of romances in general. *Spinout* casts Elvis as race car driver Mike McCoy who is also a lead singer in a rock and roll band, while *Easy Come, Easy Go* features Elvis as Navy demolitions man Ted Jackson.

In *Spinout* we once again see hints of indecisiveness in the protagonist, who this time is reluctant to compete, and as such is an evocative mix of psychological metaphors that calls to mind the trail of conscience suffered by Gary Cooper, as Sheriff Will Kane, in the definitive motion picture of the Wild West genre, *High Noon*. For both Mike McCoy and Will Kane the movie ends happily when their internal conflicts are resolved.

Easy Come, Easy Go revolves around the legend of a lost

Below: Elvis—the actor. During his years in Hollywood, Elvis' films were never given the critical recognition they deserved. *Overleaf:* Hawaiian natives comprise a large part of the cast of *Paradise Hawaiian Style*, adding to the idyllic tone of the movie.

Above: Double Trouble follows the exploits of Elvis as he weaves his way across Europe. To heighten the suspense, the plot makes use of the time-honored device of confused identities. *Clambake* uses a similar plot device, but this time it is a case of exchanged rather than mistaken identities. *Right:* Elvis as Scott Heyward in *Clambake*.

Above: **The chase suspended for the moment, Guy (Elvis) and Jill (Annette Day) can relax—briefly—in *Double Trouble*.**

treasure, and as such deals with greed. Its theme of the wages of greed echoes the powerful resolution of Dashiell Hammett's novel, *The Maltese Falcon*, itself produced as a classic motion picture by none other than Elvis Presley's own chief movie producer, Hal Wallis.

Double Trouble and *Clambake*, both released in 1967, are structured around a plot device that has been used throughout the ages, in comedies as well as tragedies— exchanged or mistaken identities. In *Double Trouble*, Elvis plays Guy Lambert, a singer who is mistakenly pursued for kidnapping and jewel theft, while in *Clambake* Elvis as millionaire Scott Heyward exchanges identities with poor water ski instructor, Tom Wilson (Will Hutchins). The plot of *Clambake* is similar to that of the opera *Martha* by Von Flotow. In both cases, there is an exchange of identities that crosses over class barriers. Both the opera and the movie end happily once the confusion of identities has been resolved. The exchange of identities acts as a device to advance the plot, but it is also symbolic of the protagonist's search for identity.

As we have noted throughout this study, the search for identity is a recurring theme in many of Elvis' movies—as well as in his personal life. The year 1968 would see another struggle emerging in Elvis, and it also would be reflected in the movies he made.

Stay Away, Joe (MGM, March 1968) is a harbinger of things to come. Like the majority of his movies, it is a light musical comedy (Elvis does, after all, sing to a bull), but the personable and polished young man of the earlier musicals has become a rougher character. Elvis as Joe Lightcloud smokes, drinks, fights and does his share of womanizing—which is definitely a different Elvis than the Elvis of the mid-1960s. Although there were always plenty of girls in his films of that period, Elvis never played a womanizer. His characters were fun-loving, but never callous in their attitudes toward women. In *Stay Away, Joe*, Elvis has become like Lord Byron's heartless, reptilian *Don Juan*, whose every love is at first unaware of his 'poison through her spirit creeping.'

The next two movies, *Speedway* (MGM, June 1968) and *Live a Little, Love a Little* (MGM, October 1968), return to the well-established pattern. In *Speedway*, Elvis is again cast as a race car driver possessed of the daring nonchalance that was so memorably evinced by Robert Mitchum's archetypal moonshine-running hillbilly in the epochal 1958 motion picture, *Thunder Road*. With action galore, plenty of songs and pretty girls, it was the type of role that his fans loved to see him in. *Live a Little, Love a Little* continues in the same vein as the other musicals. Elvis plays a fashion photographer whose personal and professional life is complicated by

Below: Speedway, **another high action musical, features Elvis as a race car driver. Given Elvis' fascination with cars, motorcycles and go-carts, this is a role for which he was particularly well suited.**

Left: As Joe Lightcloud in *Stay Away, Joe*, Elvis plays a harsher character than he had previously. A change is definitely in the air. The year *Stay Away, Joe* was released—1968—marked Elvis' triumphant return to live performing. *Below:* Elvis with Michelle Carey in *Live a Little, Love a Little*.

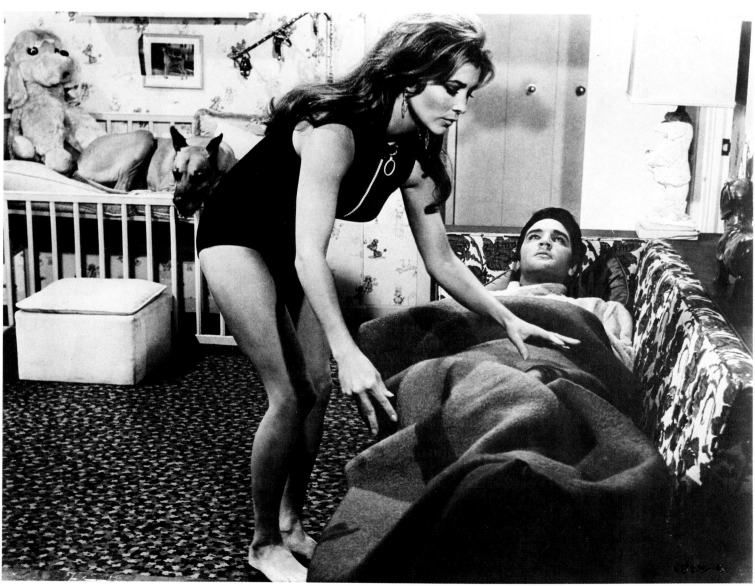

a series of odd twists. Although he would continue to make more movies of this sort, Elvis was ready for a change and his next film is a definite step in a new direction.

L ike *GI Blues* nine years earlier, *Charro!* (National General Productions, Inc., September 1969) marks another turning point in Elvis' film career. Following a period of light-hearted musicals, *Charro!* is a serious western, with Elvis playing Jess Wade, a reformed outlaw who saves a town from his former gang—yet another echo of the classic *High Noon* (see *Spinout*). This theme of the bad man turned good shares its rich resonance with the Biblical tale of the Prodigal Son, and equally reflects the intensity of the turnabout that takes place in Nicholai Gogol's tale of a young man turned against his tribe, *Taras Bulba*. Of course, the overwhelming odds with which Jess Wade is faced also partake of the heroic story of King David as a shepherd boy, when he faced the heavily armed, giant warrior Goliath with just a sling for a weapon.

The movie's one and only song plays during the credits. An even more striking change is Elvis' appearance; in contrast to the clean-living, clean-shaven movie persona of his previous films, we see a brutish, bearded Elvis. The beard—rich in the symbolism of faded youth—forces us to take a closer look at Elvis. He has at this point reached an age that is almost 10 years beyond the average life expectancy during

As the 1960s drew to a close Elvis was ready to move in a new direction. Note the contrast between the clean-shaven Elvis of the musicals of the 1960s *(facing page)* and the bearded Elvis of *Charro!* *(above)* at the end of the decade.

Above: Elvis and his leading lady in a publicity still from *Charro!*
Facing page: Like the shepherd David facing Goliath, Jess Wade is confronted with seemingly overwhelming odds.

the height of the Roman Empire. At 34 he is old and is looking down the tunnel of life, wondering whether the light at the end of the tunnel is an oncoming train. Confronted with this realization of his own mortality, Elvis left Hollywood behind him.

Although he would make two more feature films (*The Trouble With Girls and How to Get Into It* and *A Change of Habit*) after *Charro!*, the seeds of change were sown with his *NBC TV Special*. After eight years of movies, eight years of seclusion at Graceland, Elvis was ready to return to the stage. On 3 December 1968 the King of Rock and Roll returned triumphantly. Taped in June 1968—not long after the birth of his daughter Lisa Marie—the *NBC TV Special* resurrected his long dormant singing career. Although Elvis had continued to release albums during his Hollywood years, almost all were soundtracks from his movies—only three albums contained original, non-film material.

The Elvis of the *TV Special* was an Elvis that had not been seen for sometime. Clad in black leather, he was sexy and dynamic. He took to the stage with an assurance as resolute as the seventeenth-century British poet Robert Herrick, when that author penned these lines in his poem, *The Pillar of Fame*: 'This pillar never shall/Decline or waste at all/But stand forever by his own/Firm and well-fixed foundation.'

Left: The King returns! On 3 December 1968, NBC broadcast Elvis' television special. If he was worried about performing after his long absence from the stage, it never showed. His loyal subjects clustered near him, eager for his return and savoring every moment. *Below:* No one can sing a love song like the King of Rock and Roll.

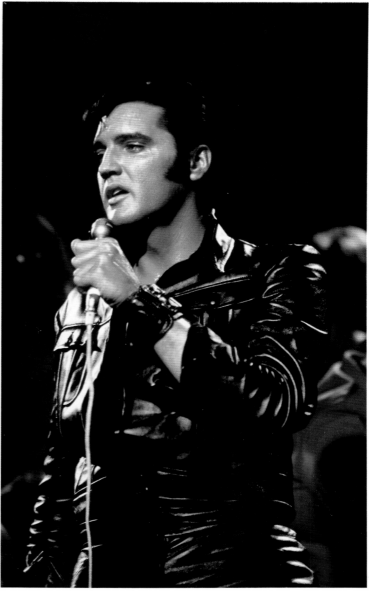

These pages: **The King could do it all, and the *NBC TV Special* showed his many facets. Underneath his many moods, Elvis was driven by a raw energy that ignited the stage and electrified the audience.**

Elvis generously poured forth his talent as lavishly as Herrick was wont to write tomes in praise of dinners he had been invited to—and Herrick, like Elvis, was always re-invited! There was an energy, an edge to the 'new Elvis' that was missing from the polished movie persona. It had been years since he had performed, but it was an art he had not forgotten and had in fact perfected.

Soon it would be Las Vegas. The success of his 1968 television special gave Elvis the incentive to return to performing live. On 26 July 1969, Elvis opened a month-long stay at the International Hotel, which set the course for his return to performing. Like the hero Prometheus, freed from the rock of the eternal torment in Shelley's *Prometheus Unbound*, he sprang to vibrant life.

The King was back indeed, but something had changed, and how fitting that metamorphosis should take place in Las Vegas, that surreal city of bright lights poised on the edge of the desert. As Samuel Taylor Coleridge said in his immortal poem, *Kubla Khan*: 'In Xanadu did Kubla Kan/a stately pleasure dome decree....'

Elvis was older now, and so was his audience. Elvis' last live performance was on 26 March 1961 at Pearl Harbor's Bloch Arena. Then he was a young and vigorous 26; now he was 34. The past beckons, but it can never be recaptured completely, and Elvis had the wisdom to know not to try, nor did he want to—rather, like a creature from Ovid's Roman classic *Metamorphosis*, Elvis became yet a newer, and more fantastic aspect of himself. Adorned in capes, wide belts of

elaborate design and jeweled jumpsuits, Elvis performed the hits of the past, but added ballads to his repertoire as well as a complete orchestra and soul singers. The raw animal magnetism of the 1950s was thus transformed into a glitzy, glittery show of lights. And it was a show never to be forgotten.

After a decade of romantic comedies, he had gone full circle and returned, in a sense, to his musical roots. Hollywood, however, was not forgotten. From his years in Hollywood, Elvis had learned even more about showmanship. Always capable of driving his audience into a frenzy, he was even better now because he was in control. The first time he heard his fans screaming, he did not know what to do so he just kept on singing. Now the screaming was a cultivated response.

The sheer magnetism of Elvis on stage was captured with two documentaries: *Elvis: That's the Way It Is* (MGM, December 1970) and *Elvis on Tour* (MGM, 1972). He was truly larger than life now. Everything about Elvis emphasized the mythology surrounding him; everything about him was flamboyant. With his capes and his jewels, he had the aura of a superman. By now the myth had overtaken the man and all he had to do was walk out on stage. He did not need to be great—but he was.

His performing career revitalized, so too was Elvis himself. He felt better, physically and emotionally, than he had in years. It was an endless, enduring circle—the high he got

Caught up in the momentum of his *NBC TV Special*, Elvis dove full force into an almost endless schedule of touring. In June 1972, he played four nights at Madison Square Garden in New York. The first night at the Garden, he held a brief press conference *(facing page)*. Elvis on stage in New York *(below left)* and in *Elvis: That's The Way It Is*, his 1970 documentary *(below)*.

These pages: **In 1973, Elvis returned to Hawaii for another television special—*Aloha from Hawaii*. The recent years had seen a transformation. As befitting a mythological figure, with his capes and jewels, he now looms larger than life.**

from performing was translated into more energy on stage. With his lyrical ballads, he could take you to the heights of Parnassus, and with his hard-driving rock and roll he could reach inside your very soul. Those who saw him perform were awed by the excitement he generated. They would walk away from a show thinking, 'This is one of the high points in my life.'

On 14 January 1973, Elvis' *Aloha From Hawaii* special was simulcast via satellite to half a billion people in 40 countries. With bikini-clad girls lounging on a sandy white beach like an image from James Michener's *Adventures in Paradise*, the beginning of the special is also evocative of one of his paradisiacal movies. Although the charisma is undeniably there, the Elvis of the 1970s is a far cry from the Hillbilly Cat of the 1950s. Dressed in a white suit, his fingers bejeweled with large rings, Elvis looked older, but imbued with more assurance and power, like a modern-day Hermes, the all-creative legend of antiquity.

Opening with 'CC Rider' followed by 'Burnin' Love,' he still did rock and roll and the songs that had made him famous, but he mixed them with lyrical ballads. Ironically, the King of Rock and Roll was now a ballad singer; his movies had foretold the direction that his singing career would take. As he sings the ballads, romantic images and peaceful scen-

ery appear on a split screen. If the audience wanted the old Elvis they never showed it. Here was a man who understood what a crowd wanted. He would sing lovingly to one woman in the crowd, then move on to another, giving her a sweat-drenched scarf, which she would cherish all her life.

Symbolizing both the myth and the man, the stage behind him is framed with larger than life neon images of him as a guitar-toting singer and the word ELVIS in gigantic lights.

As a tribute to his roots, Elvis concludes the show with a medley of Southern anthems straight out of the American subconscious: 'Oh I wish I were/ In the Land of Cotton/Old folks there/are not forgotten/Look away/Look away/Look away, Dixieland…Glory, glory Hallelujah!/Glory, glory Hallelujah/Glory, glory Hallelujah/His truth goes marching on…Hush little baby/ Don't you cry/You know your daddy's bound to die….'

He was not without his woes, however. At times it seemed that Elvis was more like the benighted Orpheus of Greek mythology, trying literally to sing his Eurydice back from the netherworld, for Elvis' Eurydice—Priscilla—had left him on 8 August 1972, and was never to return. Their divorce was final on 9 October 1973.

Elvis on Tour won the Golden Globe Award for best documentary in 1972, but the rest of his movies had never received the critical praise which they so richly deserved.

Below: A scene from *Elvis on Tour*. Finally, Elvis was given the critical acclaim which he had been so long denied while in Hollywood. *Elvis on Tour* was awarded a Golden Globe for best documentary in 1972.

The movie critics of Hollywood never considered Elvis a serious actor and thought of his movies as low comedy. Yet with *Elvis on Tour* they began to realize that they had been wrong about Elvis for nearly two decades. *Elvis on Tour's* Golden Globe was a vain effort by the snobbish elite to make up for all they had missed on his earlier films. It was a bit like the Academy of Motion Picture Arts and Sciences giving a 1971 Oscar to the Beatles for *Let It Be* after they had been achieving monumental success with the public for years. Suddenly we realized that the critics' scorn was just jealousy tainted by fear.

In 1974 Elvis was approached by Barbra Streisand to star with her as Norman Mayne in a remake of the classic *A Star is Born*. This was the opportunity that Elvis needed to gain the critics' acceptance. The door had opened—albeit begrudgingly—with the Golden Globe Award. Elvis now stood on the threshold of winning the critical acclaim that had been denied him throughout his acting career. Elvis had the energy needed to portray Norman Mayne at the height of Mayne's career, and—as he had proven years ago in *King Creole*—he also had the range to portray Mayne in the depths of his despair. At the very least, Elvis was assured of a nomination for an Academy Award for his portrayal of Norman Mayne. Sadly, it was not to be. The Colonel objected to director Jon Peters' lack of experience and to Barbra Streisand receiving top billing over Elvis. The project was rejected, and the part went to Kris Kristofferson.

Below left: Elvis on Tour has forever captured the magnetism and the power of Elvis on stage. *Below:* Elvis always had an incredible rapport with his audience. Here, amidst the screaming throngs, he manages to make a single fan believe she is the only person in the room.

Epilogue

Though scorned by the critics, all of Elvis' films were incredibly popular with the public. Elvis Presley's 33 films grossed more than $180 million for their producers. In spite of their light-hearted romantic flavor—and perhaps because of it—the movies did serve a purpose. Let it not be forgotten that the plays of William Shakespeare were written and performed to entertain the masses, and that is exactly what Elvis Presley's movies did.

Elvis is the American Dream realized one-hundredfold, but he never forgot who he was. He is and always will be the one and only King of Rock and Roll, and he will always be one of us, just a southern boy, the son of Gladys and Vernon Presley.

Elvis Presley died on 16 August 1977. He was 42.

The King was dead. This was no ordinary man who had died; and as in the days of old when a country's every move and every mood was dictated by the power behind the throne, the tempo of life was suddenly—irrevocably—changed.

The world was stunned, and then filled with disbelief. When celebrities die they are remembered for their achievements and missed by those who knew and admired them, but Elvis' death had a far greater impact. His death sent shock waves through the nation. Telephone and telegraph operators in Memphis were deluged with so many calls and telegraphs that hundreds of extra workers had to be called in. His fans were unwilling to let him go, and so the myth persisted: they would not let him die. It would seem that we needed the myth almost more than we needed the man.

Then the rumors started. Reports of Elvis being alive began to appear in newspapers and magazines. At first he was seen in Kalamazoo, Michigan; later he was spotted in Peoria, Illinois and then on a farm near Birmingham,

Facing page: **Elvis had returned to live performing, but before we knew it, he was gone forever. On 16 August 1977, the King of Rock and Roll died. Long live the King.**

Above: Elvis, early in his career. **Facing page:** At Graceland, Elvis could always find peace and solace...and so it is today.

Alabama. Throughout his life Elvis was 'larger than life,' and so it continues to be after his death. He is now trapped between death and an eternal life on earth. We cannot touch him physically yet neither can we let him go.

World literature is full of resurrection myths, from the biblical tale of Lazarus to the legend of the Phoenix, the bird that rises reborn from the ashes of its funeral pyre. Elvis is the Phoenix, and we are all experiencing his glorious rebirth.

Who is Elvis? Is he a man or a myth?

The myth of Elvis transcends the man—He has become immortal.

Index